U[N]
C O M M O N
S E N S E

◆

COWBOY LOGIC, QUIPS AND QUOTES
AND TRUE POLITICAL CORRECTNESS

◆

BY TOM SMILEY

Uncommon Common Sense consists of quips and quotes and other material that I have accumulated over years of public speaking. I have very limited knowledge of the origins of such quips and quotes. I assume no personal credit for much of the material found in *Uncommon Common Sense*. I am simply attempting to repeat that which I have heard from various sources over many, many years. When at all possible, I have tried my best to give acknowledgement and credit to my sources as best I can recall. I will gladly make any corrections or additions in future editions. Any opinions or assumptions, whether political or otherwise, should not be attributed to any group or individuals with whom I am acquainted professionally or personally. The Proverbs come from the Holy Bible, several various translations.

UNCOMMON COMMON SENSE
© 2011 by Tom Smiley

Published by
LIFE WITH SMILES MINISTRY
P.O. BOX 81
GAINESVILLE, GA 30503
www.LifeWithSmiles.com
tsmiley@LakewoodLife.org

Printed and bound in the United States of America

ISBN 978-1-4507-6438-4

TABLE OF CONTENTS

DEDICATION

Uncommon Common Sense; Cowboy Logic, Quips and Quotes, and True Political Correctness is dedicated in loving memory of Keith Rochester (1939 - 2004).

Each week John McKibbon, Joe Wood, Jr. and I would meet with Keith for prayer and accountability.

Keith always provided us three "younger" guys with great wisdom and insight about life, marriage, children, business, and faith. We especially miss his constant reminder, accompanied by his grin, "your kids will be fine, look at mine."

We miss Keith and are indebted to his "uncommon common sense, quips and quotes, and true political correctness."

We are pleased to provide financial resources to publish this book in his memory.

John McKibbon, Joe Wood, Jr., Tom Smiley
2011

Acknowledgements

I would like to express appreciation:

To my faithful wife, Terri, who was unselfish in her assistance in editing and proofing the manuscript.

To Mike and Jill Schenden for their faithful financial and technical support of Life with Smiles Ministry.

To Anne Davenport and her fine staff at Matthews Printing. Anne and her team were invaluable in assisting me in making decisions regarding *Uncommon Common Sense* becoming a reality.

To Phil Hudgins for his kind foreward and assistance.

To my Administrative Assistant, Amanda Stowers, for working to get *Uncommon Common Sense* ready for publication.

To the entire staff at Lakewood Baptist Church for offering suggestions, ideas and constructive criticism during the writing phase.

To Jacobs Media and Al Gainey for allowing me to "test" the thoughts, opinions and logic of *Uncommon Common Sense*.

To John McKibbon and Joe Wood, Jr. for their encouragement to write something in honor of Keith Rochester.

Tom Smiley

FOREWORD

If folks ever decide to *roast* Tom Smiley and they're looking for stories that describe him, all they have to do is talk to his hunting buddies—and his Mama.

Let's start with Mama, better known at Lakewood Baptist Church as Joann Smiley Smith. She remembers wonderful stories about Tom, some of which she can actually tell in public. For one thing, she says, Tom has always had a sense of right and wrong. Even as a youngster on school bus patrol, he did not waver from his assigned duty. So when his best friend was misbehaving on the bus, Tom reported him.

"Tom, I'm your best friend," the boy pleaded.

"When I'm a patrol on the bus, I have no friends," Tom answered.

There's one side of Dr. Thomas R. Smiley: dedicated to the task, determined to do the right thing, decisive in his actions.

And then there's Tom Smiley with a gun in his hands. Tom Smiley the hunter. Tom Smiley the fast shot. "My Bird" Smiley.

He was quick on the trigger even as a 10-year-old when his father, the late Harry Smiley, took him quail hunting in the fields around Gum Branch, Georgia, where Tom grew up. His very first quail hunt, Tom came home with eight or ten birds he had shot, his mother remembers. When Jim, his older brother, questioned how a little guy like Tom could kill that many quail on one hunt, their Daddy didn't say a word. Neither did Tom.

It was a few years later before the truth came out, Joann says. Yes, Tom bagged eight or ten quail that day. But he *shot them on the ground, not in flight.* "He just got excited and shot before he was supposed to," his mother recalls.

Good friend Rusty Hopkins says, "Today Tom is known to his hunting buddies as 'My Bird.' That's because he is so competitive—and an excellent shot." Another Friend, Gary Funk says, "He shoots fast and then worries about whose bird he just shot."

"He'll shoot, kill the bird and yell 'My bird,'" says State Sen. Butch Miller, who's been on numerous hunts with Tom, along with Rusty and Gary. "That's why we all call him 'My Bird.'" (We won't mention the time Tom shot just as the guide's dog jumped up for a low-flying bird. The dog suffered only a minor nick in one ear. There remains doubt about who shot the dog.)

So there's that side of Tom Smiley: competitive, quick and athletic, certain of what's his.

"He's not always right," Hopkins says, "but he's always certain."

One thing Tom is certain about is that Americans could use a little more common sense—*uncommon* common sense. Common sense from people like this country's founding fathers, who knew political correctness when it was really correct.

Common sense from philosophers and writers, common sense and logic from cowboys, and even common sense—if you can understand it—from the great Yogi Berra.

That's what this book, *Uncommon Common Sense,* is all about. It's a collection of easy-to-read comments and one-liners from all kinds of people. So sit back and take it in. Ponder. Enjoy. Smile.

And if we're lucky, common sense might just make a comeback.

UNCOMMON
COMMON
SENSE

❧ ❧ ❧

Including:
Yogi Said What?
Profound Thoughts Made Simple from Yogi Berra

UNCOMMON COMMON SENSE

"Every tub has to sit on its own bottom."

– *Tom Smiley*

❦ ❦ ❦

Real charity doesn't care if it is tax deductible or not.

❦ ❦ ❦

Envy is a waste of time. You already have all you need.

❦ ❦ ❦

The most important things in life are not things.

❦ ❦ ❦

Do it Now! Today will be yesterday tomorrow.

Never ask a barber if you need a haircut.

⚜ ⚜ ⚜

Plow around a stump long enough and it will rot itself out!

⚜ ⚜ ⚜

To be successful you must do these three things:
  · Show up
  · Show up on time
  · Show up dressed to play

⚜ ⚜ ⚜

"Order without liberty and liberty without order are equally destructive."

  – *Theodore Roosevelt*

⚜ ⚜ ⚜

Don't envy violent people or copy their ways.

Proverbs 3:31

"All I Really Need to Know, I Learned in Kindergarten."
- · Share everything.
- · Play fair.
- · Don't hit people.
- · Put things back where you found them.
- · Clean up your own mess.
- · Don't take things that aren't yours.
- · Say you're sorry when you hurt somebody.
- · Wash your hands before you eat.
- · Flush.
- · Warm cookies and cold milk are good for you.
- · Take a nap every afternoon.

– *Robert Fulghum*

❧ ❧ ❧

Live a balanced life - learn some and think some and draw and paint and sing and dance and play and work every day some.

❧ ❧ ❧

Save for retirement starting with your first paycheck.

Life is too short to waste time hating anyone.

∞ ∞ ∞

Your job won't take care of you when you are sick.
Your friends and parents will. Stay in touch.

∞ ∞ ∞

Pay off your credit cards every month.

∞ ∞ ∞

Make peace with your past so it won't screw up the
present.

∞ ∞ ∞

If a relationship has to be a
secret, you shouldn't be in it.

Avoid all
perverse talk;
stay away from
corrupt speech.
Proverbs 4:24

∞ ∞ ∞

Everything can change in the blink of an eye. But don't worry; God never blinks.

ᐧᕈᐧ ᐧᕈᐧ ᐧᕈᐧ

It's never too late to have a happy childhood. But the second one is up to you and no one else.

ᐧᕈᐧ ᐧᕈᐧ ᐧᕈᐧ

When it comes to going after what you love in life, don't take no for an answer.

ᐧᕈᐧ ᐧᕈᐧ ᐧᕈᐧ

Time heals almost everything. Give time, time.

ᐧᕈᐧ ᐧᕈᐧ ᐧᕈᐧ

However good or bad a situation is, it will change.

ᐧᕈᐧ ᐧᕈᐧ ᐧᕈᐧ

Believe in miracles.

ᶜᵒ ᶜᵒ ᶜᵒ

Don't wait for your ship to come in if you haven't sent one out.

ᶜᵒ ᶜᵒ ᶜᵒ

What you give lives.

ᶜᵒ ᶜᵒ ᶜᵒ

Before you set your heart on something, look around you and see how happy people are who have it.

ᶜᵒ ᶜᵒ ᶜᵒ

There are two theories to arguing with a woman. Neither one works.

Tainted wealth
has no lasting
value, but right
living can save
your life.
Proverbs 10:2

If duct tape can't fix it, it ain't broke.

❧ ❧ ❧

The only thing achieved without effort is failure.

❧ ❧ ❧

"Not everything that can be counted counts, and not everything that counts can be counted."

– *Albert Einstein*

❧ ❧ ❧

Do not resent growing old. Many are denied the privilege.

"Even if you are on the right track, you will get run over if you just sit there."

– *Will Rogers*

❧ ❧ ❧

"You should never live according to what you lack."

– *Nick Vujicic*

❦❦ ❦❦ ❦❦

"No matter what you've done for yourself or for humanity, if you can't look back on having given love and attention to your own family, what have you really accomplished?"

– *Lee Iacocca*

❦❦ ❦❦ ❦❦

"No success in public life can compensate for failure in the home."

– *Benjamin Disraeli*

❦❦ ❦❦ ❦❦

One thing you can give and still keep is your word.

Too much talk leads to sin. Be sensible and keep your mouth shut.

Proverbs 10:19

❦❦ ❦❦ ❦❦

Never part without loving words. They might be your last.

❧ ❧ ❧

People may forget how fast you did a job, but they will remember how well you did it.

❧ ❧ ❧

Probably a man's most profitable words are those spent praising his wife.

❧ ❧ ❧

"Don't sin by letting anger control you. Think about it overnight and remain silent."

  – Psalm 1:4

❧ ❧ ❧

Your ship would come in much sooner if you would swim out to meet it.

There is always time to add a word, never to withdraw one.

᚛ᚑ ᚛ᚑ ᚛ᚑ

Thanksgiving was never meant to be shut up in a single day.

᚛ᚑ ᚛ᚑ ᚛ᚑ

I cannot give you the formula for success, but I can give you the formula for failure:
Try to please everybody.

᚛ᚑ ᚛ᚑ ᚛ᚑ

Without wise leadership, a nation falls; there is safety in having many advisers.
Proverbs 11:14

YOGI SAID, WHAT?
Profound Thoughts Made Simple from Yogi Berra

A nickel ain't worth a dime anymore.

ズ ズ ズ

All pitchers are liars or crybabies.

ズ ズ ズ

Always go to other people's funerals, otherwise they won't come to yours.

ズ ズ ズ

Baseball is ninety percent mental and the other half is physical.

ズ ズ ズ

Even Napoleon had his Watergate.

ズ ズ ズ

Half the lies they tell about me aren't true.

He hits from both sides of the plate. He's amphibious.

ⅩⅩⅩ

How can you think and hit at the same time?

ⅩⅩⅩ

I always thought that record would stand until it was broken.

ⅩⅩⅩ

I just want to thank everyone who made this day necessary.

ⅩⅩⅩ

I never said most of the things I said.

ⅩⅩⅩ

I think Little League is wonderful. It keeps the kids out of the house.

I wish I had an answer to that because I'm tired of answering that question.

I'm not going to buy my kids an encyclopedia. Let them walk to school like I did.

If you ask me anything I don't know, I'm not going to answer.

This is like deja vu all over again.

You can observe a lot just by watching.

"He must have made that before he died."

– *Referring to a Steve McQueen movie*

𝄇 𝄇 𝄇

You've got to be very careful if you don't know where you're going, because you might not get there.

𝄇 𝄇 𝄇

I knew I was going to take the wrong train, so I left early.

𝄇 𝄇 𝄇

If you can't imitate him, don't copy him.

𝄇 𝄇 𝄇

You better cut the pizza in four pieces because I'm not hungry enough to eat six.

𝄇 𝄇 𝄇

It was impossible to get a conversation going;
everybody was talking too much.

Slump? I ain't in no slump. I just ain't hitting.

Nobody goes there anymore; it's too crowded.

It gets late early out there.

 - *Referring to the bad sun conditions in left
   field at the stadium.*

"Do you mean now?"

 - *When asked for the time.*

"I take a two hour nap, from one o'clock to four."

𝕏 𝕏 𝕏

"If you come to a fork in the road, take it."

𝕏 𝕏 𝕏

"You give 100 percent in the first half of the game, and if that isn't enough in the second half you give what's left."

𝕏 𝕏 𝕏

"I made a wrong mistake."

𝕏 𝕏 𝕏

"Yeah, but we're making great time!"

  – *In reply to "Hey Yogi, I think we're lost."*

𝕏 𝕏 𝕏

"Why buy good luggage? You only use it when you travel."

🏃 🏃 🏃

"The other teams could make trouble for us if they win."

🏃 🏃 🏃

"He can run anytime he wants. I'm giving him the red light."

– On the acquisition of fleet Rickey Henderson.

🏃 🏃 🏃

"It ain't the heat; it's the humility."

🏃 🏃 🏃

"The towels were so thick there I could hardly close my suitcase."

🏃 🏃 🏃

COWBOY LOGIC

Including:
Testing Your Cowboy Knowledge

The Cowboy Code

COWBOY LOGIC

"Courage is being scared to death - and saddling up anyway."

– *John Wayne*

A man can't go anywhere as long as he's straddling a fence.

Failures should be a guidepost – not a hitching post.

If you get to thinkin' you're a person of some influence, try orderin' somebody else's dog around.

Never approach a bull from the front, a horse from the rear, or a fool from any direction.

Never slap a man who's chewing tobacco.

The best way out of a difficulty is through it.

Never miss a good chance to shut up.

Never kick a cow chip on a hot day.

A beautiful woman who lacks discretion is like a gold ring in a pig's snout.

Proverbs 11:22

Men are best measured by what they finish, not by what they attempt.

To hatch despair, just brood over your troubles.

Don't let life discourage you, everyone who got where he is had to begin where he was.

Pray not for lighter loads but for stronger backs.

May God grant me the determination and tenacity of a weed.

A closed mouth gathers no foot.

Many people are so filled with fear that they go through life running from something that isn't after them.

Lettin' the cat outta the bag is a whole lot easier'n puttin' it back.

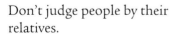

Doing beats stewing.

Don't judge people by their relatives.

The generous will prosper; those who refresh others will themselves be refreshed.
Proverbs 11:25

Behind every successful rancher is a wife who works in town.

When you lose, don't lose the lesson.

Talk slowly, think quickly.

Remember that silence is sometimes the best answer.

Live a good, honorable life. Then when you get older and think back, you'll enjoy it a second time.

Don't interfere with something that ain't botherin' you none.

The easiest way to eat crow is while it's still warm.

If you find yourself in a hole, the first thing to do is stop diggin'.

If it don't seem like it's worth the effort, it probably ain't.

Wealth from get-rich-quick schemes quickly disappears.

Proverbs 13:11

It don't take a genius to spot a goat in a flock of sheep.

Sometimes you get and sometimes you get got.

Generally, you ain't learnin' nothing when your mouth's a-jawin'.

Don't compare your life to others. You have no idea what their trail has been about.

What other people think of you is none of your business.

Don't take yourself so seriously. No one else does.

The best kind of a cat is a dog.

If your parents never had children, chances are you won't, either.

It's not what you look at that matters, it's what you see.

The dumbest people I know are those who know it all.

A gentle answer deflects anger, but harsh words make tempers flare.

Proverbs 15:1

Common sense ain't common.

Life isn't tied with a bow, but it's still a gift.

If you climb in the saddle, be ready for the ride.

It is easier to get an actor to be a cowboy than to get a cowboy to be an actor.

Boots, chaps and cowboy hats.... nothing else matters.

The quickest way to double your money is to fold it over and put it back into your pocket.

If you are facing in the right direction, all that's left for you to do is keep on walking.

Real Men Don't Make War On Women!

Fast is good but accurate is better.

Don't just lay there and bleed.

Never corner something meaner than you.

Plans go wrong for lack of advice; many advisers bring success.

Proverbs 15:22

Sure you can trust the Government, ask any Indian.

Don't stop kicken till the clock stops ticken.

Success depends on your backbone, not your wishbone.

Your fences need to be horse-high, pig-tight and bull-strong.

Meanness don't jes' happen overnight.

It don't take a very big person to carry a grudge.

You cannot unsay a cruel word.

Every path has a few puddles.

Don't pick a fight with an old man. If he is too old to fight, he'll just kill you.

Let sleeping dogs lie.

You don't sow and reap the same day.

A lazy person is as bad as someone who destroys things.
Proverbs 18:9

When you're thirsty it's too late to think about digging the well.

There's one thing for which you can be thankful—only you and God have all the facts about yourself.

Too many folks are more interested in the honey than they are the bees who produce.

An upright man can never be a downright failure.

A dog is smarter than some people. It wags its tail and not its tongue.

TESTING YOUR COWBOY KNOWLEDGE

Match the proper word to each cowboy term.

(Answers on page 48)

_____ Skunk Eggs

_____ Pecos, Strawberries, Whistle Berries

_____ Hot Rocks, Soda Sinkers, Shotgun Waddin'

_____ Lick, Larrup

_____ Slow Elk

_____ Splatter Dabs, Wheelers

_____ Brown Gargle

_____ Texas Butter

_____ Cowboy who rides a bucking bronc solely by balancing himself in the saddle

_____ Spurring a bronc's sides first with one foot and then with the other

_____ To lose a stirrup

_____ To grasp the saddle horn while contest bronc riding

_____ A bronc that reverses its position in the middle of a high buck

_____ Chaps

_____ Shallow water where cows have stood

_____ Meringue pie topping

_____ Evaporated milk

_____ Rice pudding with raisins

_____ Cook's helper, dishwasher

_____ Temporary hired hand used when ranch is short of help

_____ To admit the truth, to confess a lie, or acknowledge an obvious personal shortcoming

A. Gravy
B. Choking the Apple
C. Calf Slobber
D. Beans
E. Bicycling
F. Bat Wings
G. Waddy
H. Beef Tea

I. Spotted Pup
J. Beef
K. Canned Cow
L. Onions
M. Coffee
N. Balance Rider
O. End Swapper
P. Biscuits

Q. Acknowledge the Corn
R. Blow a Stirrup
S. Swamper
T. Molasses
U. Pancakes

THE COWBOY CODE

Never pass anyone on the trail without saying "Howdy."

———————

Never approach someone from behind without giving a shout from outside shooting range.

———————

Never wave at a man on a horse, as it might spook the horse. A nod is the proper greeting.

———————

Never try on another man's hat.

———————

Never shoot an unarmed or unwarned enemy.

Never shoot a woman, no matter what.

———————

Never go back on your word - your word is your bond, a handshake is more binding than a contract.

———————

Never wake another man by shaking or touching him, as he might wake suddenly and shoot you.

———————

"I won't be wronged. I won't be insulted. I won't be laid a-hand on. I don't do these things to other people, and I require the same from them."

  – *John Wayne as John Bernard Books in The Shootist*

Answers to Testing Your Cowboy Knowledge:
(page 45)

L. Onions
D. Beans
P. Biscuits
T. Molasses
J. Beef
U. Pancakes
M. Coffee
A. Gravy
N. Balance Rider
E. Bicycling
R. Blow a Stirrup
B. Choking the Apple
O. End Swapper
F. Bat Wings
H. Beef Tea
C. Calf Slobber
K. Canned Cow
I. Spotted Pup
S. Swamper
G. Waddy
Q. Acknowledge the Corn

QUIPS AND QUOTES

Including:
Humor's Poignant Point

Comments from 1955

Why Do We Love Children?

QUIPS AND QUOTES

The biggest troublemaker you'll probably ever have to deal with watches you shave his face in the mirror every morning.

All diseases run into one——Old Age.

"Self-made man? No such thing."
   - *John McKibbon*

We are all either fools or undiscovered geniuses.

Despite the high cost of living it remains a popular item.

"Hurtful people are usually Hurting people."

  - *Rick Warren*

Failure is success if we learn from it.

Nothing is a waste of time if you use the experience wisely.

Good judgment comes from experience, and a lot of that comes from bad judgment.

"Any man who'd make an X-rated movie ought to have to take his daughter to see it."

  - *John Wayne*

Sensible people control their temper; they earn respect by overlooking wrongs.

Proverbs 19:11

Life isn't fair, but it's still good.

⚜ ⚜ ⚜

When in doubt, just take the next small step.

⚜ ⚜ ⚜

"I got mine. How'd you do?"
  - *P. Martin Ellard*

⚜ ⚜ ⚜

Cry with someone. It's more healing than crying alone.

⚜ ⚜ ⚜

It's OK to let your children see you cry.

⚜ ⚜ ⚜

Get rid of anything that isn't useful, beautiful or joyful.

"It is what it is."

  - Joe Wood, Jr.

God loves you because of who God is, not because of anything you did or didn't do.

"The most important guest is the one right in front of you."

  - Vann M. Herring

The man who smiles when things go wrong has thought of someone to blame it on.

Those too lazy to plow in the right season will have no food at the harvest.

Proverbs 20:4

"Don't make me laugh, my lip is cracked."

- *Jack McKibbon*

It's funny that those things your kids did that got on your nerves seem so cute when your grandchildren do them.

Don't audit life. Show up and make the most of it now.

There are two reasons why we don't trust people; one, because we don't know them; and the other, because we do.

Some of the most disappointed people in the world are those who get what is coming to them.

Life is not measured by the number of breaths we take, but by the moments that take our breath away.

❧❧❧

All that truly matters in the end is that you loved.

❧❧❧

Get outside every day. Miracles are waiting everywhere.

❧❧❧

If we all threw our problems in a pile and saw everyone else's, we'd grab ours back.

❧❧❧

What the country needs is dirtier fingernails and cleaner minds.

Don't say, "I will get even for this wrong." Wait for the Lord to handle the matter.

Proverbs 20:22

"Many of life's failures are people who did not realize how close they were to success when they gave up."

– *Thomas Edison*

The odds of hitting your target go up dramatically when you aim at it.

There is no passion to be found playing small - in settling for a life that is less than the one you are capable of living.

One secret of success in life is for a man to be ready for his opportunity when it comes.

Stop leaving and you will arrive.

Stop searching and you will see.

Stop running away and you will be found.

You can't wait for inspiration, you have to go after it with a club.

It is not the length of life, but the depth of life.

A child is not a vase to be filled, but a fire to be lit.

People may be right in their own eyes, but the Lord examines their heart.

Proverbs 21:2

There area three ways to get something done: Do it yourself, hire someone to do it, or forbid your kids to do it.

We always admire the other fellow more after we have tried to do his job.

Adversity causes some men to break, others to break records.

Your character is all you have left when you've lost everything you can lose.

In times of prosperity men ask too little of God.
In times of adversity they ask too much.

Some people continue to change jobs, mates and
friends—but never think of changing themselves.

Some people change not because they see the light but
because they feel the heat.

When you are done with
changing—you're done.

The person who
strays from
common sense
will end up in the
company of the
dead.

Proverbs 21:16

Confessing your sins is no
substitute for forsaking them.

If you see a turtle on a fence post... someone put him there.

꧁꧂꧁꧂꧁꧂

The best employees work for their employers as though they were self-employed.

꧁꧂꧁꧂꧁꧂

Paradoxical Paranoia is when you believe everyone is against you and they really are.

꧁꧂꧁꧂꧁꧂

More men will fail through lack of purpose rather than lack of talent.

꧁꧂꧁꧂꧁꧂

The most important thing a father can do for his children is to love their mother.

꧁꧂꧁꧂꧁꧂

"No man is worth his salt who is not ready at all times to risk his well-being, to risk his body, to risk his life, in a great cause."

  – *Theodore Roosevelt*

"Great leadership inspires great follow-ship."

  – *Rusty Hopkins*

"Aim where they're heading, not where they are."

  – *Gary Funk*

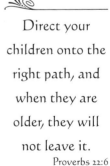

Direct your children onto the right path, and when they are older, they will not leave it.

Proverbs 22:6

Blessed are those who can give without remembering, and take without forgetting.

When it comes to giving, some people stop at nothing.

⌘⌘⌘

A difficult moment for an atheist is when he feels grateful and has no one to thank.

⌘⌘⌘

Be grateful for the doors of opportunity—and the friends who oil the hinges.

⌘⌘⌘

People are generally about as happy as they've made up their minds to be.

⌘⌘⌘

A real home is more than a roof over your head—it's a foundation under your feet.

⌘⌘⌘

Greatness is not found in possessions, power, position, or prestige. It is discovered in goodness, humility and character.

❧❧❧

Learn to speak kind words—nobody resents them.

❧❧❧

There are two kinds of bores—those who talk too much and those who listen too little.

❧❧❧

Nature's tip—your ears aren't made to shut, but your mouth is.

❧❧❧

You can't fake listening. It shows.

❧❧❧

A person without self-control is like a city with broken-down walls.

Proverbs 25:28

"You got that right."

   – *Butch Miller*

Fear more that you will not hear God rather than fear HE won't hear you.

Love will find a way, indifference will find an excuse.

Life is tragic for those who have plenty to live on and nothing to live for.

Love is more about what you do, than what you feel.

"A man who wants to lead the orchestra must turn his back on the crowd."

– *Max Lucado*

"Try not to become a man of success but a man of value."

– *Albert Einstein*

"Men do less than they ought, unless they do all they can."

– *Thomas Carlyle*

"Reputation is what men and women think of us; character is what God and angels know of us."

– *Thomas Paine*

As iron sharpens iron, so a friend sharpens a friend.

Proverbs 27:17

"The essential thing is not knowledge, but character."

  – Joseph Le Conte

"Reputation is for time; character is for eternity."

  – J. B. Gough

"The art of being wise is knowing what to overlook."

  – William James

"Shallow men believe in luck, strong men believe in cause and effect."

  – Ralph Waldo Emerson

The aim of education should be to teach us how to think, rather than what to think.

Fear not that thy life shall come to an end, but rather fear that it shall never have a beginning.

"Ministry is serious business."

– *Harry Smiley*

"One monkey don't stop the show."

– *Lois Jones*

Better to be poor and honest than to be dishonest and rich.
Proverbs 28:6

Vision is not enough, it must be combined with venture. It is not enough to stare up the steps, we must step up the stairs.

When the character of a man is not clear to you, look at his friends.

"You can make more friends in two months by becoming interested in other people than you can in two years by trying to get other people interested in you."

- *Dale Carnegie*

"No good decision was ever made in a swivel chair."

- *George S. Patton*

"My father gave me the greatest gift anyone could give another person, he believed in me."

- Jim Valvano

The parent is, and remains, the first and most important teacher that the child will ever have.

The value of marriage is not that adults produce children but that children produce adults.

The most important thing that parents can teach their children is how to get along without them.

Fearing people is a dangerous trap, but trusting the Lord means safety.

Proverbs 29:25

Don't be discouraged if your children reject your advice. Years later they will offer it to their own offspring.

⋄⋄⋄

By the time we realize our parents may have been right, we usually have children who think we're wrong.

⋄⋄⋄

"A man's life does not consist of the things he owns."

 - *Jesus*

⋄⋄⋄

Patience is a quality that is most needed when it is exhausted.

⋄⋄⋄

A great oak is only a little nut that held its ground.

There are four steps to accomplishment. Plan purposefully, prepare prayerfully, proceed positively, pursue persistently.

The last time you failed, did you stop trying because you failed—or did you fail because you stopped trying?

The world is full of willing people; some willing to work, the rest willing to let them.

One machine can do the work of fifty ordinary men. No machine can do the work of one extraordinary man.

Fire tests the purity of silver and gold, but a person is tested by being praised.

Proverbs 27:21

When you are dissatisfied and would like to go back to your youth—think of Algebra.

Opportunity has the uncanny habit of favoring those who have paid the price of years of preparation.

Freedom is a package deal—with it comes responsibilities and consequences.

No single raindrop ever thought itself responsible for the flood.

"That sounds good but it won't feed the bulldog."

- *Woodrow "Woody" Stewart*

If you want your children to keep their feet on the ground, put some responsibility on their shoulders.

The man whose ship comes in usually finds most of his relatives at the dock.

As a man grows older and wiser, he talks less and says more.

If you can't be satisfied with what you have received, be thankful for what you have escaped.

Interfering in someone else's argument is as foolish as yanking a dog's ears.

Proverbs 26:17

If a fellow isn't thankful for what he's got, he isn't likely to be thankful for what he's going to get.

Medical doctors measure physical health by how the tongue looks. The Great Physician measures spiritual health by how the tongue acts.

There's only one thing finer than a friend you can trust, and that's one who trusts you.

A lot of indigestion is caused by people having to eat their own words.

Work spares us from three great evils: Boredom, Vice and Need.

HUMOR'S POIGNANT POINT

"The more things change the more they stay the same."

I do not like this Uncle Sam,
I do not like his health care scam.
I do not like these dirty crooks,
or how they lie and cook the books.
I do not like when Congress steals,
I do not like their secret deals.
I do not like this speaker Nan ,
I do not like this 'YES, WE CAN'.
I do not like this spending spree—
I'm smart, I know that nothing's free.
I do not like your smug replies,
when I complain about your lies.
I do not like this kind of hope.
I do not like it.
Nope, Nope, Nope!

How Fights Start

My wife sat down on the settee next to me as I was flipping channels. She asked, 'What's on TV?'
I said, 'Dust.'
And then the fight started...

―――――――――

My wife was hinting about what she wanted for our upcoming anniversary.
She said, 'I want something shiny that goes from 0 to 150 in about 3 seconds.'
I bought her a bathroom scale.
And then the fight started...

―――――――――

When I got home last night, my wife demanded that I take her some place expensive... so, I took her to a gas station.
And then the fight started...

―――――――――

My wife and I were sitting at a table at my school reunion, and I kept staring at a drunken lady swigging her drink as she sat alone at a nearby table.

My wife asked, 'Do you know her?'

'Yes,' I sighed, 'She's my old girlfriend. I understand she took to drinking right after we split up those many years ago, and I hear she hasn't been sober since.'

'My goodness!' says my wife, 'who would think a person could go on celebrating that long?'

And then the fight started...

———————

I took my wife to a restaurant. The waiter, for some reason took my order first. "I'll have the steak, medium rare, please."

He said, "Aren't you worried about the mad cow?"

"Nah, she can order for herself."

And then the fight started...

———————

Top 10 Best Ever Caddie Quips

#10. Golfer: "That can't be my ball, it's too old."
Caddie: "It's been a long time since we teed off, sir."

#9. Golfer: "How should I have played that last shot?"
Caddie: "Under an assumed name."

#8. Golfer: "This is the worst golf course I ever played."
Caddie: "This isn't the golf course, we left that over an hour ago, sir!"

#7. Golfer: "I've never played this badly before."
Caddie: "I didn't realize that you had played before, sir."

#6. Golfer: "Please stop checking your watch, it is annoying."
Caddie: "This isn't a watch, sir. It is a compass."

#5. Golfer: "I've played so poorly, I think I'm going to go drown myself in that lake."
Caddie: "I don't think you could keep your head down that long."

#4. Golfer: "I'd move heaven and earth to be able to break 100."
Caddie: "Try heaven, you've already moved most of the earth."

#3. Golfer: "Do you think it is a sin to play golf on Sunday?"
Caddie: "The way you play, Sir, it's a crime any day of the week!"

#2. Golfer: "Do you think I can get there with a 5-iron?"
Caddie: "Eventually."

#1. Golfer: "You've got to be the worst caddy in the world!" he screamed.
Caddie: "I doubt it. That would be too much of a coincidence."

Quick Thinking

An elderly woman walked into the local country church. The friendly usher greeted her at the door and helped her up the flight of steps, "Where would you like to sit?" he asked politely.

"The front row please," she answered.

"You really don't want to do that," the usher said "The pastor is really boring."

"Do you happen to know who I am?" the woman inquired. "No." he said. "I'm the pastor's mother," she replied indignantly.

"Do you know who I am?" he asked. "No." she said. "Good," he answered.

Comments Made in the Year 1955!
(only 55 years ago)

"I'll tell you one thing, if things keep going the way they are, it's going to be impossible to buy a week's groceries for $20.00."

—————————

"Have you seen the new cars coming out next year? It won't be long before $2,000. 00 will only buy a used one."

—————————

"If cigarettes keep going up in price, I'm going to quit. A quarter a pack is ridiculous."

—————————

"Did you hear the post office is thinking about charging a dime just to mail a letter?"

"If they raise the minimum wage to $1.00, nobody will be able to hire outside help at the store."

"When I first started driving, who would have thought gas would someday cost 29 cents a gallon. Guess we'd be better off leaving the car in the garage."

"Kids today are impossible. Those duck tail hair cuts make it impossible to stay groomed. Next thing you know, boys will be wearing their hair as long as the girls."

"I'm afraid to send my kids to the movies any more. Ever since they let Clark Gable get by with saying Damn in *Gone with the Wind*, it seems every new movie has either Hell or Damn in it!"

"Did you see where some baseball player just signed a contract for $75,000 a year just to play ball? It wouldn't surprise me if someday they'll be making more than the President."

―――――――――

"I never thought I'd see the day all our kitchen appliances would be electric. They are even making electric typewriters now."

―――――――――

"It's too bad things are so tough nowadays. I see where a few married women are having to work to make ends meet."

―――――――――

"It won't be long before young couples are going to have to hire someone to watch their kids so they can both work."

"I'm afraid the Volkswagen car is going to open the door to a whole lot of foreign business."

———

"Thank goodness I won't live to see the day when the Government takes half our income in taxes. I sometimes wonder if we are electing the best people to congress."

———

"The drive-in restaurant is convenient in nice weather, but I seriously doubt they will ever catch on."

———

"There is no sense going to Lincoln or Omaha anymore for a weekend. It costs nearly $15.00 a night to stay in a hotel."

Why Do We Love Children?

1) Perspective...I was driving with my three young children one warm summer evening when a woman in the convertible ahead of us stood up and waved. She was stark naked! As I was reeling from the shock, I heard my 5-year-old shout from the back seat, "Mom, that lady isn't wearing a seat belt!"

2) Opinions... On the first day of school, a 1st-grader handed his teacher a note from his mother. The note read, "The opinions expressed by this child are not necessarily those of his parents."

3) Ketchup... A woman was trying hard to get the ketchup out of the jar. During her struggle the phone rang so she asked her 4-year-old daughter to answer the phone. "Mommy can't come to the phone to talk to you right now. She's hitting the bottle."

4) Innocence... A little boy got lost at the YMCA and found himself in the women's locker room. When he was spotted, the room burst into shrieks, with ladies grabbing towels and running for cover. The little boy watched in amazement and then asked, "What's the matter, haven't you ever seen a little boy before?"

5) Sincerity... While taking a routine vandalism report at an elementary school, I was interrupted by a little girl about 6-years-old. Looking up and down at my uniform, she asked, "Are you a cop?" "Yes," I answered and continued writing the report. "My mother said if I ever needed help I should ask the police. Is that right?" "Yes, that's right," I told her. "Well, then," she said as she extended her foot toward me, "would you please tie my shoe?"

6) Inquisitive... It was the end of the day when I parked my police van in front of the station. As I gathered my equipment, my K-9 partner, Jake, was barking, and I saw a little boy staring in at me. "Is that a dog you got back there?" he asked. "It sure is," I replied. Puzzled, the boy looked at me and then towards the back of the van. Finally he said, "What'd he do?"

7) Reflection... While working for an organization that delivers lunches to elderly shut-ins, I used to take my 4-year-old daughter on my afternoon rounds. She was unfailingly intrigued by the various appliances of old age, particularly the canes, walkers and wheelchairs. One day I found her staring at a pair of false teeth soaking in a glass. As I braced myself for the inevitable barrage of questions, she merely turned and whispered, "The tooth fairy will never believe this!"

8) Dress up...A little girl was watching her parents dress for a party. When she saw her dad donning his tuxedo, she warned, "Daddy, you shouldn't wear that suit." "And why not, darling?" "You know that it always gives you a headache the next morning."

9) School...A little girl had just finished her first week of school. "I'm just wasting my time," she said to her mother. "I can't read, I can't write, and they won't let me talk!"

10) Bible...A little boy opened the big family Bible. He was fascinated as he fingered thru the old pages. Suddenly, something fell out of the Bible. He picked up the object and looked at it. What he saw was an old leaf that had been pressed in between the pages. "Mama, look what I found," the boy called out. "What have you got there, dear?" With astonishment in the young boy's voice, he answered, "I think it's Adam's underwear!"

Sunday Clothes

A little boy was walking down a dirt road after church one Sunday afternoon when he came to a crossroads where he met a little girl coming from the other direction.

'Hello,' said the little boy; 'Hi,' replied the little girl.

'Where are you going?' asked the little boy.

'I've been to church this morning and I'm on my way home,' answered the little girl. 'I'm also on my way home from church. Which church do you go to?' asked the little boy.

'I go to the Baptist church back down the road,' replied the little girl. 'What about you?' 'I go to the Methodist church back at the top of the hill,' replied the little boy.

They discover that they are both going the same way so they decided that they'd walk together.

They came to a low spot in the road where spring rains had partially flooded the road, so there was no way that they could get across to the other side without getting wet.

'If I get my new Sunday dress wet, my Mom's going to skin me alive,' said the little girl.

'My Mom'll tan my hide, too, if I get my new Sunday suit wet,' replied the little boy.

'I tell you what I think I'll do,' said the little girl. 'I'm gonna pull off all my clothes and hold them over my head and wade across.'

'That's a good idea,' replied the little boy. 'I'm going to do the same thing with my suit.'

So they both undressed and waded across to the other side without getting their clothes wet. They were standing there in the sun waiting to drip dry before putting their clothes back on, when the little boy finally remarked:

'You know, I never realized before just how much difference there really is between a BAPTIST and a METHODIST!!!'

The Memorial Stone

Billy died.... His will provided $30,000 for an elaborate funeral. As the last guests departed the affair, his wife, Joyce, turned to her oldest and dearest friend, Jonelle. "Well, I'm sure Billy would be pleased," she said.

"I'm sure you're right," replied Jonelle, who lowered her voice and leaned in close.
"How much did this really cost?"

"All of it," said Joyce. "Thirty thousand dollars."

"No!" Jonelle exclaimed. "I mean, it was very nice, but $30,000?"

Joyce answered, "The funeral was $6,500. I donated $500 to the church.

The food and snacks were another $500. The rest went for the Memorial Stone."

Jonelle quickly computed the total of $7,500 and said "$22,500 for a Memorial Stone? My goodness, how big is it?"

Joyce answered, "Two and a half carats."

The Truth will Find You Out

At the University of Michigan, there were four sophomores taking chemistry and all of them had an 'A' so far. These four friends were so confident that, the weekend before finals, they decided to visit some friends and have a big party. They had a great time but, after all the hearty partying, they slept all day Sunday and didn't make it back to Ann Arbor until early Monday morning.

Rather than taking the final then, they decided that after the final they would explain to their professor why they missed it. They said that they visited friends but on the way back they had a flat tire. As a result, they missed the final. The professor agreed they could make up the final the next day. The guys were excited and relieved. They studied that night for the exam.

The next day the Professor placed them in separate rooms and gave them a test booklet. They quickly answered the first problem worth 5 points. "Cool!" they thought! Each one in separate rooms, thinking this was going to be easy... then they turned the page. On the second page was written.....................

For 95 points: Which tire? _____

Don't Ask a Question
You Don't Know the Answer To

A police officer was being cross-examined by a defense attorney during a felony trial. The lawyer was trying to undermine the police officer's credibility .....

Q: "Officer — did you see my client fleeing the scene?"
A: "No sir. But I subsequently observed a person matching the description of the offender, running several blocks away."

Q: "Officer — who provided this description?"
A: "The officer who responded to the scene."

Q: "A fellow officer provided the description of this so-called offender. Do you trust your fellow officers?"
A: "Yes, sir. With my life."

Q: "With your life? Let me ask you this then officer. Do you have a room where you change your clothes in preparation for your daily duties?"
A: "Yes sir, we do!"

Q: "And do you have a locker in the room?"
A: "Yes, sir, ... I do."

Q: "And do you have a lock on your locker?"
A: "Yes, sir."

Q: "Now, ... why is it, officer, if you trust your fellow officers with your life, you find it necessary to lock your locker in a room you share with these same officers?"

A: "You see, sir — we share the building with the court complex, and sometimes lawyers have been known to walk through that room."

The courtroom EXPLODED with laughter, and a prompt recess was called.

It's All About ME

A man and his wife walked into a dentist's office.

The man said to the dentist, "Doc, I'm in one heck of a hurry. I have two buddies sitting out in my car waiting for us to go play golf, so forget about the anesthetic, I don't have time for the gums to get numb. I just want you to pull the tooth, and be done with it!

We have a 10:00 AM tee time at the best golf course in town and it's 9:30 already... I don't have time to wait for the anesthetic to work!'

The dentist thought to himself, "My goodness, this is surely a very brave man asking to have his tooth pulled without using anything to kill the pain." So the dentist asked him, "Which tooth is it sir?"

The man turned to his wife and said, "Open your mouth Honey, and show him."

A Real "Dear"

A man and his friend were enjoying Deer Hunting Season in rural Arkansas near a blacktop highway. A huge buck walked by and the hunter carefully drew his bow and took careful aim.

Before he could release his arrow, his friend pointed at a funeral procession passing on the road below their stand. The hunter slowly let off the pressure on his bow, took off his hat, bowed his head and closed his eyes in prayer. His friend was amazed. "Wow! That is the most thoughtful and touching thing I have ever seen. You are the kindest man I have ever known.

The hunter shrugged. "Yeah, well, we were married for 35 years."

The Moral Is.......Don't Be Late

A priest was being honored at his retirement dinner after 25 years in the Parish. A leading local politician and member of the congregation was chosen to make the presentation and to give a little speech at the dinner.

However, he was delayed, so the priest decided to say his own few words while they waited.

"I got my first impression of the Parish from the first confession I heard here. I thought I had been assigned to a terrible place.

The very first person who entered my confessional told me he had embezzled money, had a hit and run accident, cheated on his Bar Exam, lied on his income tax and had stolen money from his parents.

I was horrified. But, as the days went on, I learned that my people were not all like that and I had, indeed, come to a fine Parish full of good and loving people....."

Just as the priest finished his talk, the politician arrived full of apologies at being late. He immediately began to make the presentation and gave his talk.

"I'll never forget the first day our Parish priest arrived," said the politician. "In fact, I had the honor of being the first person to go to him for confession."

TRUE POLITICAL CORRECTNESS

Including:
The Ultimate Pledge:
Life, Fortune and Sacred Honor

Amendments to the Constitution of
the United States of America

TRUE POLITICAL CORRECTNESS

In God we trust.

"The democracy will cease to exist when you take away from those who are willing to work and give to those who would not."

– *Thomas Jefferson*

"When people fear the government you have tyranny, when government fears the people you have Liberty."

– *Thomas Jefferson*

Always choose life.

"Of the four wars in my lifetime, none came about because the U.S. was too strong."

    – Ronald Reagan

No one is in charge of your happiness but you.

"Those who are too smart to engage in politics are punished by being governed by those who are dumber."

    – Plato

Good planning and hard work lead to prosperity, but hasty shortcuts lead to poverty.

Proverbs 21:5

"When I was a boy I was told that anybody could become President; I'm beginning to believe it."

    – Clarence Darrow

George Washington is the only president who didn't blame the previous administration for his troubles.

"I offer my opponents a bargain: if they will stop telling lies about us, I will stop telling the truth about them."

– *Adlai Stevenson, campaign speech, 1952*

There are always too many Democratic congressmen, too many Republican congressmen, and never enough U.S. congressmen.

"Why pay money to have your family tree traced; go into politics and your opponents will do it for you."

"Bad officials are elected by good citizens who do not vote."

– *George Jean Nathan*

"A Constitution of Government once changed from Freedom, can never be restored. Liberty, once lost, is lost forever."

– *John Adams*

"How many observe Christ's birthday! How few, His precepts! O! 'tis easier to keep Holidays than Commandments."

– *Benjamin Franklin*

Don't be impressed with your wisdom. Instead, fear the Lord and turn away from evil.

Proverbs 3:7

"A fondness for power is implanted, in most men, and it is natural to abuse it, when acquired."

   – *Alexander Hamilton*

"Duty is ours; results are God's."

   – *John Quincy Adams*

"Don't hit at all if it is honorably possible to avoid hitting; but never hit soft."

   – *Theodore Roosevelt*

"Is life so dear or peace so sweet as to be purchased at the price of chains and slavery? Forbid it, Almighty God! I know not what course others may take, but as for me, give me liberty or give me death!"

   – *Patrick Henry*

"The only sure bulwark of continuing liberty is a government strong enough to protect the interests of the people, and a people strong enough and well enough informed to maintain its sovereign control over the government."

– *Franklin D. Roosevelt*

"Eternal vigilance is the price of liberty."

– *Wendell Phillips*

"Restriction of free thought and free speech is the most dangerous of all subversions. It is the one un-American act that could most easily defeat us."

– *William O. Douglas*

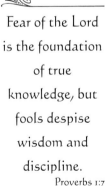

Fear of the Lord is the foundation of true knowledge, but fools despise wisdom and discipline.

Proverbs 1:7

"When they call the roll in the Senate, the Senators do not know whether to answer "Present" or "Not guilty.""

– *Theodore Roosevelt*

"You cannot help the poor
By destroying the rich.
You cannot strengthen the weak
By weakening the strong.
You cannot bring about prosperity
By discouraging thrift.
You cannot lift the wage earner up
By pulling the wage payer down.
You cannot further the brotherhood of man
By inciting class hatred.
You cannot build character and courage
By taking away people's initiative and independence.
You cannot help people permanently
By doing for them,
What they could and should do for themselves."

– *Abraham Lincoln*

"We must not mind insulting men, if by respecting them we insult God."

– Chrysostom, the Archbishop of Constantinople

"They that can give up essential liberty to obtain a little temporary safety, deserve neither liberty nor safety."

– Benjamin Franklin

"Timid men prefer the calm of despotism to the tempestuous sea of Liberty."

– Thomas Jefferson

The Lord directs our steps, so why try to understand everything along the way?

Proverbs 20:24

"I think we have more machinery of government than is necessary, too many parasites living on the labor of the industrious."

– Thomas Jefferson

"The principle of spending money to be paid by posterity, under the name of funding, is but swindling futurity on a large scale."

– *Thomas Jefferson*

"Before a standing army can rule, the people must be disarmed; as they are in almost every kingdom of Europe. The supreme power in America cannot enforce unjust laws by the sword; because the whole body of the people are armed, and constitute a force superior to any band of regular troops that can be, on any pretence, raised in the United States."

– *Noah Webster*

"A nation of well informed men who have been taught to know and prize the rights which God has given them cannot be enslaved. It is in the region of ignorance that tyranny begins."

– *Benjamin Franklin*

No one has ever devised a method by which the public can get something out of government for nothing.

"It is impossible for the man of pious reflection not to perceive in [the Constitution] a finger of that Almighty hand which has been so frequently and signally extended to our relief in the critical stages of the revolution."

– James Madison

Democracy, like love, can survive almost any attack—except neglect and indifference.

A good leader inspires men to have confidence in him; a great leader inspires them to have confidence in themselves.

Trust in the Lord with all your heart; do not depend on your own understanding.

Proverbs 3:5

Just because the Declaration of Independence says everyone is entitled to the pursuit of happiness, it doesn't mean the government should finance the cause.

There comes a time when a nation must choose between tightening the belt or losing the pants.

Government is not the greatest institution in the world, rather it is the human family.

"A people that values its privileges above its principles soon loses both."

– *Dwight D. Eisenhower*

"If we desire to secure peace, it must be known that we are at all times ready for war."

 – *George Washington*

"Make us to see that our liberty is the right to do as we please, but the opportunity to do right."

 – *Peter Marshall, in U.S. Senate Prayer*

"To live under the American Constitution is the greatest political privilege God ever gave to mankind."

 – *Calvin Coolidge*

Do not withhold good from those who deserve it when it's in your power to help them.

Proverbs 3:27

"A dread disease is gnawing at the basic structure of American existence—the home. There is but one ray of hope—God!"

 – *J. Edgar Hoover*

Our government has continued to grow until big government threatens to become, not the government of the people, but in place of the people.

"America does not consist of groups. A man who thinks of himself as belonging to a particular national group in America has not yet become an American."

– *Woodrow Wilson*

Democracy is based upon the conviction that there are extraordinary possiblitities in ordinary people.

"America was born a Christian nation for the purpose of exemplifying unto the nations of the world the principles of righteousness found in the Revelation of God."

– *Woodrow Wilson*

"If we abide by the principles taught in the Bible, our country will go on prospering. But if we and our posterity neglect its instruction and authority, no man can tell how suddenly a catastrophe may overwhelm us and bury our glory in profound obscurity."

– *Daniel Webster*

"Firearms are second only to the Constitution in importance; they are the peoples' liberty teeth."

– *George Washington*

"In the final choice a soldier's pack is not so heavy as a prisoner's chains."

– *Dwight D. Eisenhower*

Don't pick a fight without reason, when no one has done you harm.

Proverbs 3:30

"Though the people support the government; the government should not support the people."

– *Grover Cleveland*

"The Bible is the rock on which this Republic rests."

– *Andrew Jackson*

"I tremble for my country when I reflect that God is just; that His justice cannot sleep forever."

– *Thomas Jefferson*

"Let every nation know, whether it wishes us well or ill, that we shall pay any price, bear any burden, meet any hardship, support any friend, oppose any foe to assure the survival and the success of liberty."

– *John F. Kennedy*

"We can have no "50-50" allegiance in this country. Either a man is an American and nothing else, or he is not an American at all."

   – *Theodore Roosevelt*

"It is impossible to rightly govern a nation without God and the Bible."

   – *George Washington*

"And so, my fellow Americans, ask not what your country can do for you; ask what you can do for your country."

   – *John F. Kennedy*

Choose a good reputation over great riches; being held in high esteem is better than silver or gold.

Proverbs 22:1

"I have one yardstick by which I test every major problem - and that yardstick is: Is it good for America?"

   – Dwight D. Eisenhower

"If your actions inspire others to dream more, learn more, do more and become more, you are a leader."

   – John Quincy Adams

"I predict future happiness for Americans if they can prevent the government from wasting the labors of the people under the pretense of taking care of them."

   – Thomas Jefferson

The rich think of their wealth as a strong defense; they imagine it to be a high wall of safety.

Proverbs 18:11

"My reading of history convinces me that most bad government results from too much government."

– *Thomas Jefferson*

"The strongest reason for the people to retain the right to keep and bear arms is, as a last resort, to protect themselves against tyranny in government."

– *Thomas Jefferson*

Trust in the Lord with all your heart; do not depend on your own understanding.

Proverbs 3:5

"To compel a man to subsidize with his taxes the propagation of ideas which he disbelieves and abhors is sinful and tyrannical."

– *Thomas Jefferson*

John F. Kennedy held a dinner in the White House for a group of the brightest minds in the nation at that time. He made this statement: "This is perhaps the assembly of the most intelligence ever to gather at one time in the White House with the exception of when Thomas Jefferson dined alone."

"In the decades to come, when Islam becomes the majority in England, France, and Greece will Christians be afforded special considerations and concessions as Muslims are today?"

– *Tom Smiley*

"The reflection upon my situation and that of this army produces many an uneasy hour when all around me are wrapped in sleep. Few people know the predicament we are in."

– *George Washington, letter to Joseph Reed, January 14, 1776*

We can make our plans, but the Lord determines our steps.

Proverbs 16:9

Almost all of us long for peace and freedom; but very few of us have much enthusiasm for the thoughts, feelings, and actions that make for peace and freedom.

The secret of a well crafted political speech is to have a good beginning and a good ending; and to have the two as close together as possible.

"Then join hand in hand, brave Americans all! By uniting we stand, by dividing we fall!"

– *John Dickinson, The Liberty Song, 1768*

"The die is cast. The people have passed the river and cut away the bridge."

– *John Adams, writing about the Boston Tea Party, December, 1773*

Wise words are more valuable than much gold and many rubies.

Proverbs 20:15

"Sink or swim, live or die, survive or perish, I am with my country from this day on. You may depend on it."

– *John Adams, letter to a friend, 1774*

"I am not a Virginian, but an American."

– *Patrick Henry, Speech from the First Continental Congress, October 14, 1774*

"In the language of the Holy Writ, there is a time for all things. There is a time to preach and a time to fight and now is the time to fight."

– *John Peter Gabriel Muhlenberg, spoken to his congregation in 1775 before leaving to join General Washington's troops in Virginia*

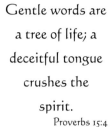

Gentle words are a tree of life; a deceitful tongue crushes the spirit.

Proverbs 15:4

"I am well aware of the toil and blood and treasure that it will cost to maintain this Declaration, and support and defend these States. Yet through all the gloom I can see the rays of ravishing light and glory. I can see that the end is worth more than the means."

– *John Adams, letter to Abigial Adams, July 3, 1776*

★ ★ ★

"I only regret that I have but one life to lose for my country."

– *Captain Nathan Hale, twenty-one-year-old soldier who was captured behind enemy lines while on reconnaissance for George Washington and hanged by the British, 1776*

★ ★ ★

"We hold these truths to be self-evident; that all men are created equal; that they are endowed by their Creator with certain unalienable rights; that among these are life, liberty, and the pursuit of happiness."

–*Thomas Jefferson, The Declaration of Independence, July 4, 1776*

You can make plans, but the Lord's purpose will prevail.

Proverb 19:21

"I have lived, Sir, a long time, and the longer I live, the more convincing proofs I see of this truth—that God governs the affairs of men. And if a sparrow cannot fall to the ground without His notice, is it probable that an empire can rise without His aid?"

– *Benjamin Franklin, Constitutional Convention,*
  September 1787

"Our Constitution was made only for a moral and religious people. It is wholly inadequate to the government of any other."

– *John Adams to the Officers of the First Brigade of the 3rd*
  Division of the Massachusetts Militia,
  October 11, 1798

"To the memory of the Man, first in war, first in peace, and first in the hearts of his countrymen."

– *Henry Lee, from his Eulogy of*
  George Washington, December 1799

Work brings profit, but mere talk leads to poverty.

Proverbs 14:23

"Those who expect to reap the blessings of freedom must, like men, undergo the fatigue of supporting it."

– *Thomas Paine, The American Crisis, No. 4,*
September 12, 1777

"In times of peace the people look most to their representatives; but in war, to the executive solely."

– *Thomas Jefferson, letter to Caesar A. Rodney,*
February 10, 1810

"I agree with you that in politics the middle way is none at all."

– *John Adams, letter to Horatio Gates,*
March 23, 1776

Honor the Lord with your wealth and with the best part of everything you produce.

Proverbs 3:9

"It is in the man of piety and inward principle, that we may expect to find the uncorrupted patriot, the useful citizen, and the invincible soldier. God grant that in America true religion and civil liberty may be inseparable and that the unjust attempts to destroy the one, may in the issue tend to the support and establishment of both."

 – *John Witherspoon, from his sermon on May 17, 1776*

"Gentlemen, you will permit me to put on my spectacles, for, I have grown not only gray, but almost blind in the service of my country."

 – *George Washington, searching for his glasses before delivering the Newburgh Address, March 15, 1783*

"To lengthen thy life lessen thy meals."

 – *Benjamin Franklin, Poor Richard's Almanack, October 1733*

"Think of three things; whence you came, where you are going, and to whom you mustaccount."

– *Benjamin Franklin, Poor Richard's Almanack, 1755*

"The Iraqi forces are conducting the Mother of all Retreats."

– *Dick Cheney*

A fool is
quick-tempered,
but a wise person
stays calm when
insulted.
Proverbs 12:16

The Utimate Pledge:
Life, Fortune and Sacred Honor

Believe me, dear Sir: there is not in the British empire a man who more cordially loves a union with Great Britain than I do. But, by the God that made me, I will cease to exist before I yield to a connection on such terms as the British Parliament propose; and in this, I think I speak the sentiments of America.

– by Thomas Jefferson, November 29, 1775

John Adams (1735-1826) was a teacher, farmer, and a lawyer by trade. He was driven into the Revolutionary movement by the Stamp Act and soon found himself consumed with the cause of the patriots. Adams was a member of Continental Congress (1774 to 1778) and a key figure in getting George Washington's appointment for commander and chief of the Continental Army. He was the first Vice President; and the second President of the United States. He died at the age of 91, on the same day as Thomas Jefferson, July 4, 1826, fifty years after signing the Declaration of Independence.

Samuel Adams (1722-1803) found his calling as an expert instigator and organizer of propaganda and colonial resistance during the Revolutionary period. Adams was a member of Continental Congress (1774-1775). He was elected to Lieutenant Governor, interim Governor, and Governor of Massachusetts.

Charles Carroll (1737-1832) was barred from public life for nearly a decade because of his Roman Catholic faith. In the 1770's Carroll became a champion for the Revolutionary cause through his newspaper writings, and was a prominent player in the movement from then on. He was also the only Roman Catholic to sign the Declaration of Independence. Living to the age of 95, he became the last surviving signer of the Declaration of Independence.

Benjamin Franklin (1706-1790) was largely self-taught. Upon his return from Europe in 1775, he became a member of the Continental Congress (1775), and was on the committee that drafted the Declaration of Independence. Franklin returned to Europe as a diplomat and was instrumental in garnering French aid and military assistance during the War.

John Dickinson (1732-1808) is known as the Penman of the Revolution for his influential work entitled *Letters from a Farmer in Pennsylvania* in which he refuted Great Britain's right to taxation of the colonies. Dickinson did not vote in favor of the Declaration of Independence in 1776, though he supported the cause of independence during the War and thereafter.

Nathan Hale (1755-1776) A Connecticut-born school teacher, he volunteered for an espionage mission, was caught by the British in Manhattan, and hanged following the battle of Long Island.

George Mason (1725-1792) was a delegate to the Constitutional Convention but failed to sign the Constitution out of criticism that it failed to effectively protect citizen's rights. Mason advocated that Congress adopt the Bill of Rights and is considered the "Father of the Bill of Rights," as the principal author of the document.

Alexander Hamilton (1757-1804) was a member of Continental Congress (1782, 1783, 1787, 1788) and an organizer of the Constitutional Convention. He authored 51 of the 85 *Federalist Papers*, which were enormously influential in achieving ratification of the Constitution. Hamilton was killed in a duel with Aaron Burr in 1804.

John Witherspoon (1723-1794) was a Scottish-born clergyman. Advocating resistance to the Crown in his sermons, essays, and addresses, he became involved in the Revolutionary movement and was member of Continental Congress (1776 to 1779, 1780 to 1781, 1782); was a signer of the Declaration of Independence.

Patrick Henry (1736-1799) was a member of the Virginia House of Burgesses; member of Continental Congress (1775, 1776, 1783 to 1785). He was primary drafter of the Declaration of Independence. Jefferson went on to become Vice President, and third President of the United States. He died at the age of 83 only hours before the death of John Adams on July 4, 1826, the 50th anniversary of the adoption of the Declaration of Independence.

John Jay (1745-1829) was the Governor of New York; one of the negotiators of the Treaty of Paris; and was appointed by George Washington as the first Chief Justice of the U.S. Supreme Court.

Henry Lee (1756-1818) was known as "Light-horse Harry," he was an unsurpassed cavalry commander during the Continental Congress (1785 to 1788); Governor of Virginia; and a member of the U.S. House of Representatives. Lee was also the father of Robert E. Lee.

John Peter Gabriel Muhlenberg (1746-1707) in 1775, he famously finished his sermon and left to join Washington's troops. Muhlenberg served throughout the War and was promoted to the rank of Major General. He later served as both a U.S. Congressman and Senator.

John Paul Jones (1747-1792) was the first man assigned the rank of First Lieutenant in the Continental Navy and is known as the "Father of the American Navy." Jones record of naval victories earned him the Gold Medal by Congress in 1787.

Thomas Paine (1737-1809) His pamphlet series entitled *The American Crisis* and signed "Common Sense" was highly influential in furthering the cause for American independence. After being banned from England for treason and imprisoned and nearly executed in Paris as an Englishman, Paine returned to America at the invitation of President Thomas Jefferson but lived his remaining years in poverty and isolation.

James Madison (1751-1836) was a member of the
Virginia legislature; member of Constitutional Congress
(1780-1783); delegate to the Constitutional Convention;
U.S. Congressman; Secretary of State; and 4th President
of the United States. Madison is known as the "Father of
the Constitution," and was the chief architect of the
document. As a member of the first U.S. Congress, he
sponsored the Bill of Rights. As Secretary of State, he
engineered the Louisiana Purchase of 1803. As
President, he successfully led the country through the
War of 1812.

John Marshall (1755-1835) was a captain in the Revo-
lutionary War and served with George Washington at
Valley Forge. Marshall was Chief Justice of the Supreme
Court, a position that he held for 34 years.

Benjamin Rush (1745-1813) was a member of
Continental Congress (1776,1777); signer of the
Declaration of Independence; Surgeon General of the
Continental Army; and Treasurer of U'S' Mint. Rush set
up the first free medical clinic and later helped to found
the first American anti-slavery society.

George Washington (1732-1799) in 1754, he was commissioned as a lieutenant colonel and fought in the French & Indian War from 1755 to 1758, whereupon he retired to Mount Vernon to live the life of a gentleman farmer. Washington was elected to command all Continental armies in June of 1775 and led the successful campaign against the British that ultimately forced their surrender on October 19, 1781. He was unanimously chosen as the first President under the new Constitution. Washington died at the age of 67 from a severe throat infection on the night of December 14, 1799.

We hold these truths to be self-evident, that all men are created equal, that they are endowed by their Creator with certain unalienable Rights, that among these are Life, Liberty and the pursuit of Happiness.

— The United States Declaration of Independence

Amendments to Constitution of the United States of America

The Constitution of the United States of America was officially adopted on 17th September, 1787, at the Federal Convention in Philadelphia, Pennsylvania.

Since then it has been amended 27 times and can be amended in the future as well.

The procedure for amending the constitution as described in Article V involves two parts.

The first part is the proposal of the amendments by a vote of two-thirds majority in both houses of the Congress.

The second part is the ratification of the proposed amendment, that is, it should be approved by three-fourths of states or a majority vote of the state legislatures.

Of the 27 amendments, the first 10 were ratified together. They are known as the Bill of Rights. The other 17 were subsequently ratified. The 27 amendments to the US constitution are as follows:

Amendments 1 - 10: Bill of Rights (Ratified on 12/15/1791.)

Amendment 1: Protects the freedom of religion, speech, and the press, as well as the right to assemble and petition the government.

Amendment 2: Protects the right to keep and bear arms.

Amendment 3: Quartering of soldiers prohibited during peacetime. Soldiers should be quartered at a civilian home only with the owners permission.

Amendment 4: Prohibits unreasonable searches and seizures and sets out requirements for search warrants based on probable cause.

Amendment 5: Prohibits trial for a crime except on indictment of a Grand Jury and double jeopardy, prohibits punishment without legal procedures and taking away of private property without adequate compensation.

Amendment 6: Protects the right to a fair and speedy public trial by jury, including the rights to be notified of the accusations, to confront the accuser, to obtain witnesses and to retain counsel.

Amendment 7: Right to trial by a jury in civil cases.

Amendment 8: Prohibits excessive fines and excessive bail, as well as cruel and unusual punishment.

Amendment 9: Assures the recognition of those rights that people may have but are not listed here.

Amendment 10: Limits the powers of the federal government to those delegated to it by the Constitution.

Amendments 11 - 27

Amendment 11: Immunity of states from suits from out-of-state citizens and foreigners not living within the state borders. Lays the foundation for sovereign immunity.

Amendment 12: Specifies the procedure for electing the President and the Vice-President of the US separately by ballot votes.

Amendment 13: Establishes the abolishment of slavery from the US and all the places that fall under its jurisdiction.

Amendment 14: Broadly defines the parameters of the US citizenship, prohibits the states from reducing or diminishing the privileges of citizens and emphasizes their 'right to due process and the equal protection of the law.'

Amendment 15: The citizens' right to vote shall not be denied by the states or the federal government on the basis of race, color or previous status of servitude.

Amendment 16: Allows the federal government to collect **income tax.**

Amendment 17: Establishes the direct election of the senators to the United States Senate.

Amendment 18: Establishes **Prohibition of alcohol.** *(Repealed by* ***Twenty-first Amendment****)*

Amendment 19: Establishes that the citizens' right to vote shall not be denied on the basis of their gender or sex. Ratified on 8/18/1920.

Amendment 20: Fixes the dates of term commencements for Congress (January 3) and the President (January 20); known as the "**lame duck** amendment."

Amendment 21: Repeals the 18th Amendment. Prohibits the importation of intoxicating beverages. Ratified on 12/5/1933.

Amendment 22: Limits the President to two terms, or a maximum of 10 years (i.e., if a Vice President serves not more than one half of a President's term, he can be elected to a further two terms.)

Amendment 23: Allows the representation of the District of Columbia in the **Presidential elections**.

Amendment 24: Prohibits the non-payment of poll tax or other tax as a basis of denial of the right to vote.

Amendment 25: The Vice President shall become President in case the President is removed from office or in case of his death.

Amendment 26: Prohibits the federal government or the state from denying any citizen who is 18 years or above, the right to vote.

Amendment 27: Prevents laws affecting Congressional salary from taking effect until the beginning of the next session of Congress.

PERSONAL NOTES & REFLECTIONS

_____

_____

_____

_____

_____

_____

_____

_____

_____

_____

_____

_____

_____

_____

_____

_____

_____

_____